A Difference of Opinion

"Maybe we should sell the ring and use the money to get something we can use now."

Jessica stared at her. "No way! What could be better than a diamond ring?"

"But Mom won't even let us wear it," Elizabeth reminded her.

Jessica pouted. "We're supposed to agree, Liz. You should agree with me."

"Why? *You* could agree with *me*," Elizabeth said.

They looked at one another in silence. One of them had to give in, but which one?

Bantam Skylark Books in the
SWEET VALLEY KIDS series

SWEET VALLEY KIDS

JESSICA'S UNBURIED TREASURE

Written by
Molly Mia Stewart

Created by
FRANCINE PASCAL

Illustrated by
Ying-Hwa Hu

A BANTAM SKYLARK BOOK®
NEW YORK • TORONTO • LONDON • SYDNEY • AUCKLAND

RL 2, 005–008

JESSICA'S UNBURIED TREASURE
A Bantam Skylark Book / July 1992

*Sweet Valley High® and Sweet Valley Kids are
trademarks of Francine Pascal*

Conceived by Francine Pascal

*Produced by Daniel Weiss Associates, Inc.
33 West 17th Street
New York, NY 10011*

Cover art by Susan Tang

ISBN 0-553-15926-7

Published simultaneously in the United States and Canada

PRINTED IN THE UNITED STATES OF AMERICA
OPM   0 9 8 7 6 5 4 3 2 1

To Alexander Ribner

CHAPTER 1

Ready for Takeoff

"Giddy-up!" Jessica Wakefield yelled as she galloped around the bedroom on an imaginary mule.

Her twin sister, Elizabeth, pulled a pair of make-believe reins. "Whoa, slow down," she said to her own imaginary mule. "I don't want to fall over the edge of the Grand Canyon!" She galloped out the door and bumped into her mother.

Mrs. Wakefield laughed and steered Elizabeth back into the bedroom. "If you two can get off your mules, I'll help you finish packing for our trip. We leave for the airport in just a few minutes."

Elizabeth stopped playing and pointed to a small suitcase on her bed. "We're finished. We put our clothes and koala bears into the same suitcase. We're going to share everything else."

Being twins meant that Elizabeth and Jessica shared many things. One thing they shared was their looks. Both girls had blue-green eyes and long blond hair with bangs. When they dressed alike, it was almost impossible to tell them apart.

The twins didn't share all the same interests, though. Elizabeth enjoyed reading books and making up adventure games. Jessica preferred playing with her dolls and stuffed animals. But liking different things

2

didn't stop Elizabeth and Jessica from being best friends.

"I'm all packed!" the twins' older brother Steven announced as he came into their room with his suitcase. "This time I even remembered my toothbrush."

"Oh! I forgot mine," Jessica said.

Elizabeth patted their suitcase. "I packed it for you."

"Then it looks as if we're all set," Mrs. Wakefield said. "Come on downstairs. It's almost time to go."

An hour later, the Wakefields were at the large window in the waiting area, watching planes take off and land.

"Flight one-thirty-six for Flagstaff, Arizona, is now boarding at gate two," came an announcement on the loudspeaker. "First-class passengers and families with children may begin boarding now."

"That's us," Mr. Wakefield said. "Come on."

Elizabeth and Jessica ran to be first in line. A man in an airline uniform stood at the gateway. His name tag read "Martin Brown." "Hello," he greeted the twins. "You two look very excited. Is this your first time on a plane?"

"Yes," Jessica told him. "We're going on a camping trip to the Grand Canyon."

"You'll love it. I've been there many times myself," Mr. Brown said with a smile.

The next few minutes were a bustle of activity. The Wakefields boarded the plane and found their seats. Elizabeth, Jessica, and

Mrs. Wakefield were sitting together, and Steven and Mr. Wakefield were in the row right behind them.

Elizabeth sat down in the window seat, while Mr. and Mrs. Wakefield put their carryon luggage in an overhead compartment. "You can sit next to the window on the way back," Elizabeth told her sister.

"OK," Jessica replied, sitting down in the middle seat.

Mrs. Wakefield sat down and showed the twins how to buckle their seat belts.

A moment later a flight attendant stopped beside their seats. "Would you girls like a blanket?" she asked the twins.

"Can we share one?" Jessica asked.

"We share everything," Elizabeth explained.

The flight attendant smiled. "Of course you can," she said, handing them a red blanket.

"I thought you girls might like a souvenir from the flight," Martin Brown said, coming up behind the flight attendant. He handed each twin a silver pin shaped like an airplane. "The pins look just like the plane we're flying today."

"Thank you," Elizabeth and Jessica said together. They pinned the pins on their T-shirts.

"Welcome to flight one-thirty-six," a woman's voice said over the intercom. "I'm Captain Lucy Gaines. I hope you enjoy your flight with us. Please prepare for takeoff."

Elizabeth grabbed Jessica's hand as the engines started and the plane began to move. "Here we go!"

CHAPTER 2

The Grand Canyon

"We're at the Grand Canyon!" Jessica shouted as she stepped off the shuttle bus that had picked up the Wakefields and some other visitors at the airport.

The parking lot was full of people taking pictures and looking out over the railings. When Jessica and Elizabeth ran to the guardrail, they couldn't believe their eyes. The Grand Canyon stretched away into the distance as far as the eye could see in both directions. It was even wider than Elizabeth had imagined. The rocky sides of the canyon

were striped in beautiful shades of red, brown, and yellow, and birds circled high above.

"Totally awesome," Steven said, leaning over the guardrail. "I read that it's a whole mile deep."

Mr. and Mrs. Wakefield went to sign in for the trip down into the canyon. A group of visitors, led by several experienced guides, was going to camp on the bottom of the canyon. The guides had organized the trip and were in charge of the pack mules and meals. The person leading the expedition was named Mr. Frost.

Jessica knew that the campers' food, camping equipment, and suitcases would be carried down the steep trails by a mule train. The campers were going to hike down after the mules and set up their camp when they reached the bottom. From there, they would take short hikes and go rafting on the river. She could hardly wait.

Elizabeth noticed a postcard rack in front of a nearby souvenir stand. "I want to buy a postcard to send to Grandma and Grandpa before we start down," she said.

"Me, too," Jessica said.

They rushed over and twirled the rack around. There were postcards showing many different scenes. At the same moment, Jessica and Elizabeth pointed to a picture of a mule.

"I'm getting that one," they both said at once.

Elizabeth laughed. "Let's just get one

postcard, and both write on it," she suggested.

"Good idea," Jessica agreed. "We'll share it."

"Come on, girls," Mrs. Wakefield called. "We're getting ready to go."

Jessica quickly paid the vendor out of her allowance money, and then she and Elizabeth ran to join the others. Besides the Wakefields, the group included some young couples, several sets of friends, a family with three teenage girls, and an older woman traveling alone.

The older woman introduced herself to the twins. "My name is Mrs. Lambert," she said. "I have twin granddaughters about your age, and a twin brother back home in Montana."

"I'm Jessica, and this is Elizabeth," Jessica said. "We have a brother, too, but he's older." She pointed in Steven's direction. "He's a pain."

Mrs. Lambert smiled. "I know how that is," she said. "My brother was a terror. Actually, he *still* is."

Jessica and Elizabeth laughed. "We can't wait to ride the mules," Elizabeth said.

"Neither can I," Mrs. Lambert replied. "But we'll have to wait until we're at the bottom of the canyon to do that."

Nearby, Mr. Frost was supervising his assistants, Kevin and Pat, as they loaded the pack mules. They were tying suitcases onto the mules' backs with elastic cords.

"Come on, let's go watch," Jessica sug-

14

gested. Elizabeth agreed. The twins said good-bye to Mrs. Lambert and ran over.

"Do they have names?" Jessica asked as she petted a mule's soft, fuzzy nose.

"Of course they do. The one you're petting is called Sugar Lump," Kevin said.

"Attention, everybody!" Mr. Frost called out. The campers gathered around him to listen. "The mule train will go first, so Kevin and Pat can get the tents set up by the time we arrive, around dinnertime. It's a hot day and the hike is long and steep, so take it easy. You can stop to rest any time you need to. Is everyone ready?"

"Ready!" Jessica and Elizabeth said at the same time.

They watched the mules start down the

trail. In a moment, the mule train was out of sight around a large rock formation.

"Now it's our turn," Elizabeth said to her sister. "Let's go!"

CHAPTER 3

Two of a Kind

When Elizabeth awoke the next morning, she wasn't sure where she was. Then she remembered. She was in a tent at the bottom of the Grand Canyon. She had a fuzzy memory of arriving at the camp at sunset, sitting down, and falling asleep against a rock. Somebody must have carried her into the tent and put her in her sleeping bag.

"How did we get here?" Jessica mumbled from beside Elizabeth. She sat up in her sleeping bag and rubbed her eyes.

"We were so tired from hiking we fell

asleep," Elizabeth said. She wiggled her toes. Her feet were still sore from the day before.

Steven wasn't awake yet. His sleeping bag was pulled up over his head. Mr. and Mrs. Wakefield's sleeping bags were empty.

"Let's get up," Jessica said. "I'm starved."

They opened the tent flaps and looked out. The tents were arranged in a circle around a large campfire. Several people were sitting or standing near the fire, drinking cups of steaming coffee. Beyond the circle of tents was the Colorado River, which sparkled in the bright morning sunlight.

"Rise and shine!" Mr. Wakefield called out when he saw the twins. "Don't waste this beautiful morning sleeping!"

After a delicious breakfast of pancakes and bacon, Mr. Frost explained the plan for the day. There were twenty-four people in all, and they were going to divide into three groups. The groups would take turns rafting down the river and riding back to camp on the mules. The Wakefields' group was going rafting on the second day. They would spend the first day exploring the canyon near the camp.

Elizabeth was a little bit disappointed not to be going downriver right away, but she decided it would be just as much fun to explore and see what kinds of animals lived in the canyon. She waved to Mrs. Lambert, who was boarding the raft with the first group.

"Come on, let's climb up to that ledge. We'll be able to see everything from up there," Steven suggested, pointing to a wide rock shelf that overlooked the camp.

The twins agreed. "Just be careful, and don't wander too far from camp," Mr. Wakefield said.

"We'll be careful," Jessica promised.

The twins and Steven said good-bye to their parents and started toward the ledge. As she climbed, Elizabeth looked up at the sides of the canyon towering above them. "Look! It's a goat!" she said. A mountain goat was standing on a narrow ledge twenty feet up, gazing down at them. Suddenly, it turned and scampered from rock to rock up the step canyon wall.

"He must have suction cups for feet," Steven said.

A few minutes later Jessica, Elizabeth, and Steven reached the wide ledge. As she leaned against a boulder to rest, Elizabeth

heard a chirping sound. A small, furry face stared around a rock at her.

"Look, it's a chipmunk," Jessica whispered. "Isn't it cute?"

Elizabeth held her breath as the small, striped animal scurried up onto a ledge near their heads, sat up, and watched them with bright, curious eyes. Then it turned and whisked away into a hole.

"Check out those hawks flying up there," Steven said, looking up. He spread his arms out at his side and pretended to glide just like the birds of prey. "I bet they dive for fish in the river."

For the next two hours, the twins and Steven explored the rocks around their camp. By lunchtime, they were starving again. They ran back to camp full of news.

"We saw tons of animals," Jessica told Kevin as he handed them cups of juice. "Squirrels, bluebirds, goats—"

"And some really interesting bugs," Elizabeth finished for her.

Jessica made a face. "I didn't like those."

"I liked all of it," Elizabeth said. "Now we have a lot to tell Grandma and Grandpa. Let's write our postcard."

"Good idea," Jessica said. "I'll go get the card and a pen." She got up and ran to their tent and returned a moment later. "What should we say?" she asked, handing Elizabeth the pen.

"Let's start with, 'Dear Grandma and Grandpa,'" Elizabeth said. She lay the postcard on a flat rock and began writing. "'We're in the Grand Canyon—'"

"'Having lunch,'" Jessica broke in.

"That's what I was going to say," Elizabeth said. "'We went exploring and saw—'"

"'A goat and a chipmunk,'" Jessica broke in.

"That's what I was going to say," Elizabeth said again.

"Do you always agree?" Kevin asked.

"*Almost* always," Jessica and Elizabeth said at the same time. They both laughed at Kevin's surprised expression.

"It's because—" Elizabeth began.

"We're twins!" Jessica finished.

CHAPTER 4

Riding the Rapids

Early the next morning, Kevin helped the second group get ready to go rafting. He was going to be the leader for the trip downriver. Besides the Wakefields, two young women were in the group. Their names were Allison and Meg.

"Only bring what you need for one night," Kevin suggested. "But be sure you have a whole change of clothes. You're going to get wet."

"Wet?" Jessica repeated. She looked at the river. "Are we going to fall in?"

"Oh, no. Don't worry," said Allison. "We'll get splashed a lot, but you won't go overboard. It's a lot of fun—you'll see."

"Have you been rafting before?" Elizabeth asked Allison.

"Yes," Allison said. "I go a lot as part of my research."

"What kind of research?" Elizabeth asked.

"I'm a computer programmer," Allison said. "I'm creating a video game about white water rafting."

Steven looked interested. "I love playing video games," he said. "It must be great to invent them for a living."

"Come on, everybody, put on your life preservers, get your gear stowed, and find seats," Kevin said. "I'll be sitting in the back and steering."

26

"I want to sit back there, too," Jessica said, smiling at him.

"So do I," Elizabeth said.

"Sorry, but there are just two seats," Kevin told them. "Only one of you can sit with me."

"I called it first," Jessica said stubbornly.

Kevin laughed and shook his head. "I thought you two agreed on everything!" he said.

Jessica and Elizabeth looked at each other. "Well, not always," Elizabeth admitted.

"Why don't you girls take turns sitting next to Kevin," Mr. Wakefield suggested. "Jessica can go first."

After a few last-minute adjustments, the raft was ready to go. Jessica fastened the straps on her life preserver and sat down in her seat.

"We're off," Kevin said, pushing the raft away from the shore with a large paddle.

At first, they floated along in a quiet, calm stretch of water. Then Jessica could feel the river current tugging the raft quickly away from shore. "This is great!" she said, her eyes wide.

"Take a look at the canyon wall over there," Kevin said. "See those horizontal stripes of color? That's layer after layer of sand and mud that has built up over millions of years. It took millions more years for the Colorado River to carve its way through all that rock to make the canyon. And it's still hard at work," he added as a piece of the muddy shoreline crumbled and fell into the water.

Steven leaned over the edge of the raft and

dangled his hand in the water. "It's cold," he said.

Jessica dipped one finger in. "You mean freezing. I hope we don't get splashed too much."

"Oh, really?" Steven said with a devilish smile. He scooped up some water in his hand and splashed it at Jessica.

Jessica screamed and pretended to be angry, but she couldn't stop smiling. Rafting was already a lot of fun, and they had only just begun. Elizabeth was talking to Allison about computers, and Mr. and Mrs. Wakefield were talking to Allison's friend Meg. Jessica sat back and tried to count the stripes in the canyon wall.

"Look!" Elizabeth said a little while later. "It's the first group!"

Jessica looked where her sister was pointing. The people who had rafted downriver on the first day were heading back to camp on mules. Everyone in the raft waved, and the people on shore waved back.

"OK, folks, listen up," Kevin said a few minutes later. "The water is going to get rough pretty soon. There are straps on the sides of the raft to hang onto. It's fun, but I have to warn you—you're going to get wet!"

The roar of the water grew louder as the raft continued down the river. Soon the water turned white and foamy, and the raft shot through the rapids. Jessica held onto the straps with all her might.

"Wheeeeee!" Elizabeth screamed.

"Wheeee-ack!" Jessica gasped as water

splashed over the side of the boat and hit her in the face.

"I told you you'd get wet!" Kevin yelled, as he busily steered the raft around boulders.

The white water rapids lasted for what seemed like hours to Jessica. She had never done anything so exciting in her whole life. But she was glad when they finally came to some quiet water again and Kevin steered the raft toward shore. It had been a little scary, too.

"Time for lunch," Kevin said as he pushed his wet hair out of his eyes. "You'd better all change into some dry clothes before you get a chill. The rest of the way won't be as rough."

"Good," Jessica said with a breathless laugh. "I feel like I just went swimming with my clothes on!"

CHAPTER 5

Unburied Treasure

After lunch, it was Elizabeth's turn to sit in the back of the raft with Kevin. He even let her steer once through a slow, peaceful bend in the river. Elizabeth felt as though she could go on rafting forever.

"It's getting chilly," Jessica said as the sun slipped behind the rim of the canyon.

"It's because we're down so far," Mr. Wakefield explained. "The sun only shines here for a little while. At the top of the canyon, it's still very hot."

"We'll reach our landing site soon," Kevin

said. "Then we'll pitch our tents and start dinner. A nice big campfire should warm everybody up."

A few minutes later they rounded another bend in the river and a wide, flat beach came into sight.

"Here we are," Kevin said as he steered toward it. The raft bumped against some rocks and scraped bottom. Elizabeth and Jessica jumped out onto the shore to help Kevin and their father pull the raft out of the river.

"It feels good to stretch my legs," Meg said as she picked up her knapsack.

"My feet were starting to fall asleep," Steven said. "I guess it's time to do some climbing. Let's climb that boulder that sticks out into the water."

"You always want to climb boulders," Elizabeth teased. "Do you have rocks in your head?"

Steven stuck out his tongue at her and started running. "I'm going to be king of the mountain," he yelled.

"Oh, no you aren't!" Elizabeth shouted after him. She grabbed Jessica's hand. "Come on!"

Steven was ahead, climbing up onto the large rock. When he reached its flat top, he stood up and raised his fists over his head in victory.

"The winner! King of the mountain!" he called out, hopping from foot to foot.

"Let's kick him off," Jessica said, beginning to climb.

Elizabeth nodded and climbed up next to her. She and Jessica reached the top at the same moment.

"Don't come another step," Steven warned them, pretending to hold out a sword. "I'll fight you both at once. On guard." He waved his imaginary sword at the twins and lunged at them.

Elizabeth stepped back and lost her balance. "Whoooooaaaa!" she cried, grabbing at Jessica to steady herself.

"Help!" Jessica shrieked as she lost her balance, too.

Together, Elizabeth and Jessica tumbled off the rock and landed side by side on their hands and knees in the gravel.

"Ha, ha, ha!" Steven crowed. "I'm still king!"

Elizabeth and Jessica weren't paying any attention to their brother. They were both staring in astonishment at a sparkling object that lay between them on the ground.

Elizabeth blinked to make sure she was seeing clearly. "I can't believe it. It's a—"

"Diamond ring!" Jessica finished.

CHAPTER 6

Finders Keepers

"Come over here! Hurry!" Elizabeth shouted, jumping up and waving both hands over her head.

"What's wrong? Are you hurt?" Mr. Wakefield asked. He dropped the tent poles and raced over. Mrs. Wakefield was right behind him.

"What happened?" Steven asked, jumping down from the rock.

Jessica stood up, holding the diamond ring in her palm. Her eyes were wide with amazement. "Look what we found!" she said.

"We fell off the rock and found this ring on the ground," Elizabeth explained. "We both saw it at the same time."

"It's like finding buried treasure," Jessica said. "Only we didn't have to dig."

"What's going on?" Kevin asked, hurrying over.

Mrs. Wakefield picked up the ring and stared at it in disbelief. It was a woman's gold ring with a large diamond twinkling in the center. "The girls found this ring," she said.

"Can we keep it?" Jessica asked, standing on tiptoe to see it better. Even though the canyon was in shadow, the diamond sparkled like ice. Jessica thought it was the most beautiful ring in the world.

"Well," Mrs. Wakefield said, glancing at

her husband. "I guess it's finders keepers."

"Losers weepers," Steven added.

"And I'm sure the loser is very upset," Mr. Wakefield said. "This is a very valuable diamond ring. We should try to find out who the owner is."

Kevin nodded. "I'll check with Lost and Found after we go back up the trail. But thousands of people come through this canyon every year. That ring might have been lost days, weeks, or even months ago. The owner may not even have reported it lost. So there's a good chance you'll be able to keep it."

Jessica was already imagining what it would be like to tell her friends in Sweet Valley that she and Elizabeth owned a real diamond ring. Her friend Lila Fowler received a large allowance, and her parents bought her new clothes whenever she wanted, but even Lila didn't have a real gold ring with a beautiful diamond in it.

"Can I try it on, Mom, please?" Jessica begged. She took the ring from her mother and tried it on all ten of her fingers, but it was too large.

"I can't believe we found a real diamond ring," Elizabeth said.

"And it's ours to keep," Jessica added.

"That's assuming we don't find the owner," Mr. Wakefield reminded them. "And if we don't, we could sell the ring and give you girls the money to share. After all, you're really too young to wear something like this.

You might lose it. But you could use the money to buy something that both of you could enjoy."

"But we want to keep it," Jessica said, trying the ring on her middle finger again. "Isn't it the most beautiful thing you ever saw?"

"It certainly is very pretty," Mrs. Wakefield agreed. "But if you decide to keep it, I can't let you wear it until you're much older. I promise I'll find a safe place for it, though. And I'll let you look at it from time to time."

"OK," Jessica said.

Elizabeth was looking at the ring without speaking.

"Is that what you want to do, too, Elizabeth?" Mr. Wakefield asked.

Elizabeth shrugged. "I don't know."

"Well, you don't have to decide right now. But you'll both have to agree, since you both found it," Mrs. Wakefield said.

Jessica laughed. "We can always agree in the end," she said, smiling at her twin. "Right?"

"Right," Elizabeth said slowly, still looking at the ring.

Jessica grinned. She knew they would get to keep the ring. She couldn't wait to tell Lila.

CHAPTER 7

Disagreement

Elizabeth took a sip of water from her canteen and glanced over at her sister. Jessica was showing off the diamond ring to Allison and Meg.

The ring was very beautiful, Elizabeth thought, but she didn't want to wear it. It would make much more sense to sell it, as their father had suggested. Then they could buy something expensive that they both wanted or even save the money for another time.

"What are you thinking about?" Allison

asked, walking over with a bag of trail mix. She tossed some raisins and peanuts into her mouth.

"I was just wondering how much a computer would cost," Elizabeth said. She looked up at Allison. "The kind we could have at our house."

"Not as much as you would get for the ring," Allison said. "You would have plenty left over for software programs and extra things." She offered Elizabeth some trail mix. "Does Jessica like computers, too?"

Elizabeth nibbled on a peanut. "I'm not sure. She likes to play video games."

"Why don't you ask her," Allison suggested. "Go on."

"OK," Elizabeth said with a sigh. She was nervous about what Jessica would say, but she

48

decided to ask her right away and get it over with. She walked over to her sister, who had just sat down by the edge of the river. "Hi."

"Hi, Liz," Jessica replied in a dreamy voice. She had the ring on her middle finger, and she was turning her hand this way and that to watch the diamond sparkle.

"I was thinking about what Dad said," Elizabeth began hesitantly. "Maybe we should sell the ring and use the money to get something we can use now."

Jessica stared at her. "No way! What could be better than a diamond ring?"

"Well, a home computer could be a lot of fun," Elizabeth said. "We could use it for doing homework—"

"Yuck," Jessica interrupted. "That doesn't sound like much fun to me."

"And playing games, too," Elizabeth added. "You like doing that on the computers at school."

Jessica shook her head. "I don't want a computer. I want to be the only kid in our whole school to have a real diamond ring."

"But Mom won't even let us wear it," Elizabeth reminded her.

Jessica pouted. "We're supposed to agree, Liz. You should agree with me."

"Why? *You* could agree with *me*," Elizabeth said. She was getting more upset every minute. She hated arguing with Jessica.

"Girls, dinner's ready," Mrs. Wakefield called out.

Elizabeth and Jessica looked at one another in silence. One of them had to give in, but which one?

CHAPTER 8

Twin Trouble

Jessica wriggled out of her sleeping bag the next morning and poked her head out of the tent flap. A string of pack mules was standing nearby. Pat had brought them back late last night and right now the mules were patiently chewing hay.

"Good morning, Jessica," Mr. Wakefield called out. The rest of the family was already up, sitting around the camp fire. Elizabeth was talking to Allison about computers. Jessica felt grumpy as she watched them. She didn't know why Elizabeth still couldn't see how much better it would be to have a diamond ring than a boring old computer.

"Elizabeth says you two are thinking about selling the ring and buying a home computer," Mrs. Wakefield said as Jessica joined them. Elizabeth looked up as her sister sat down, but she didn't say anything.

"*Liz* is thinking about it. *I* still want to keep the ring," Jessica grumbled.

"I see," their father said. "I have to say that I think Elizabeth's idea is very practical."

"Well, I saw the ring first," Jessica said.

Elizabeth gasped. "We saw it at the same time!"

"Now, now, let's not bicker," Mrs. Wakefield cut in firmly. "I don't want this to become a sore subject."

Jessica sat back and folded her arms. She didn't have time to pout for very long, though. They had to eat breakfast, take down their tents, and load the mules for the ride back to the main camp. Soon they were ready to go.

"The mules are all strung togther," Kevin said. "So you don't even have to steer. Just sit back and enjoy the ride."

Jessica waited to see if Elizabeth would choose to ride Sugar Lump. She did. So Jessica picked a mule further up the line and climbed up onto the saddle. Elizabeth looked disappointed when she saw what Jessica was doing. But it was tough luck, Jessica said to herself. It was Elizabeth's fault for not agreeing to keep the diamond ring.

"Why don't you sell the ring and buy a big screen TV?" Steven called from behind Jessica.

"We're not going to sell it!" Jessica said with a frown.

"Let's drop the subject, please," Mr. Wakefield said impatiently.

The mule ride back to camp was supposed to be a fun trip, but Jessica wasn't enjoying herself at all. She kept glancing back to see what her sister was doing. She wished Elizabeth would change her mind.

"When we're older, we can take turns wearing it," Jessica said when they stopped for lunch later on. "I'm not trying to hog it all to myself."

"I know you're not," Elizabeth said. "But I don't want to have it at all. I think it would

be better to buy a computer, or something else we both want."

"I have the perfect solution," Steven said. "Let's just throw it into the Colorado River. Then we don't have to hear Elizabeth and Jessica argue about it anymore."

"No!" Jessica and Elizabeth both shouted.

"Well, at least you agree on *something*," their father said.

"We'll agree," Elizabeth mumbled.

Mrs. Wakefield stood up and stretched her arms. "I certainly hope so, otherwise I may just let Steven toss the ring into the river."

Jessica jumped up and walked over to her mule. She didn't know what to think. She wanted to keep the ring, and she thought it would be terrible to have to give it up.

But being angry with Elizabeth and having Elizabeth angry with her was pretty terrible, too.

CHAPTER 9

Back to Camp

Elizabeth slumped in the saddle as she rode along beside the river on Sugar Lump. Instead of having a wonderful time, she was feeling upset and hurt. She didn't know how she and Jessica would ever be able to agree.

Gazing out between her mule's ears, Elizabeth tried to concentrate. Should she be the one to give in? she wondered.

But I always give in, Elizabeth told herself. Whenever Jessica forgot to do her chores, Elizabeth did them for her. Whenever Jessica wanted to break the rules, Elizabeth always promised not to tell on her. It was time to stop giving in. Who needed a stupid old diamond ring that didn't even fit?

Finally, the mules plodded into camp. Elizabeth jumped off Sugar Lump and gave him a pat on the nose. She glanced over to see what Jessica was doing. She hoped her sister would look over and smile. Elizabeth wanted to make up and be best friends again.

But Jessica wouldn't look over. She went over and began talking to Meg.

"You look upset, Elizabeth," Mrs. Wakefield said, giving her a hug. "Can't you and Jessica reach a decision?"

Elizabeth shook her head. Then she heard a shout.

"Elizabeth, Jessica," Kevin called out. He was hurrying toward them.

"What is it, Kevin?" Mrs. Wakefield asked.

Kevin was smiling. "I just spoke to Mr. Frost. He says Mrs. Lambert lost her engagement ring the other day when they went down the river. She's a widow, and the ring has a great deal of sentimental value to her. Why don't you go show her the ring you found and see if it's the one she lost?"

"I think that's an excellent idea," Mrs. Wakefield said. She reached into her jacket pocket and pulled out the ring. "Here it is."

Jessica immediately put her hand out. "I'll carry it," she said.

"I want to carry it," Elizabeth insisted.

"If you can't even agree on who should carry it, *I'll* bring it to Mrs. Lambert," Mrs. Wakefield said firmly. "Your disagreement is becoming ridiculous!"

CHAPTER 10

Best Friends Again

Jessica walked quickly alongside her mother on the way to Mrs. Lambert's tent. She crossed her fingers behind her back. *Please let us get to keep it*, she wished silently.

"Here we are," Mrs. Wakefield said. She tapped gently on the tent pole. "Mrs. Lambert?"

"Yes?" replied a quiet voice. The tent flap zipper began to unzip, and Mrs. Lambert looked out. Her eyes were red, as if she'd been crying. "Hello," she said. "Did you have a good time rafting?"

Elizabeth and Jessica nodded.

"Mrs. Lambert, Elizabeth and Jessica found something," Mrs. Wakefield said.

"Is it yours?" Elizabeth asked as their mother opened her hand.

Jessica held her breath. Mrs. Lambert stood up, saw the ring, and instantly burst into tears. Jessica was so startled that she just stared.

"Oh, thank heaven!" Mrs. Lambert cried. She was smiling and crying at the same time. "Oh, thank you! That's my engagement ring! My husband gave it to me at our high school senior prom. Thank you so much!"

Suddenly, Jessica began crying, too. "You're welcome," she sobbed.

"Honey, why are you crying?" Mrs. Wakefield asked.

"Because Mrs. Lambert is so happy," Elizabeth explained. "Right, Jess?"

Jessica nodded and wiped her eyes. She was sorry they wouldn't get to keep the ring, but it meant she and Elizabeth didn't have a reason to argue anymore. And it made her happy to see Mrs. Lambert so overjoyed.

Mrs. Lambert put the ring back on her hand next to her wedding band. "I thought I would never see it again. I'm so grateful to you girls."

"We're just happy you have it back," Mrs. Wakefield said with a smile.

"The least I can do is give your lovely daughters a reward," Mrs. Lambert said.

"You don't have to—" Elizabeth began.

Jessica poked her in the back. "Thank you," Jessica said in her most grown-up, polite voice.

"Now, let me see." Mrs. Lambert ducked back inside her tent. A moment later she came back out with her purse. She snapped it open and pulled a crisp twenty-dollar bill from her wallet. "Thank you, girls, so very very much."

"Thank *you*," Elizabeth and Jessica said at the same time.

Jessica stared at the twenty-dollar bill. It was more money than she had ever had at once. She was already thinking of ways to spend it.

"What are you going to do with your reward?" Mr. Wakefield asked the twins when they were back at their own tent and had told him and Steven the whole story.

"Buy new dollhouse furniture," Jessica said instantly.

68

"Buy new books," Elizabeth said at the same moment.

Jessica frowned. "But I want—"

"Wait a minute," their father said, holding up his hands. "Let's not start this again!"

With a smile, he took out his wallet and removed two ten-dollar bills. "One for each of you," he said, taking the twenty-dollar bill.

Jessica looked at Elizabeth, and they both laughed. "Now we don't have to fight," Elizabeth said. She gave Jessica a hug, and Jessica hugged her back.

"Look at that." Steven pointed up at the rim of the canyon. The sun was setting behind the cliffs, and the sky was turning brilliant shades of orange and pink. "That's prettier than any old diamond anyway," Steven said.

Everybody laughed. Steven was right,

Jessica decided. And it was something they all could share.

Three days later, the Wakefields arrived back at home. A large pile of mail was waiting for them, and Mr. Wakefield looked at all the envelopes.

"Here's a letter from the Nelsons," he said. Mr. Nelson was an old friend of his from law school. He and his family lived in Oregon.

"What does it say?" Mr. Wakefield asked.

"Peter says he and Marilyn have to go to Los Angeles on business next weekend," Mr. Wakefield told her. "He wants to know if they can leave their two sons with us while they're there."

"Boys!" Jessica said. "Yuck! How old are they?"

"The last time I saw Eric and Wesley they were little babies," Mr. Wakefield said. "But they're about your age now. I'm sure you'll all have fun together."

Jessica frowned. She didn't like getting stuck with boys.

What will Eric and Wesley be like? Find out in Sweet Valley Kids #31, ELIZABETH AND JESSICA RUN AWAY.

SWEET VALLEY KIDS

Jessica and Elizabeth have had lots of adventures in *Sweet Valley High* and *Sweet Valley Twins*...now read about the twins at age seven! You'll love all the fun that comes with being seven—birthday parties, playing dress-up, class projects, putting on puppet shows and plays, losing a tooth, setting up lemonade stands, caring for animals and much more! It's all part of SWEET VALLEY KIDS. Read them all!

☐ **JESSICA AND THE SPELLING BEE SURPRISE #21**   15917-8 $2.75

☐ **SWEET VALLEY SLUMBER PARTY #22**   15934-8 $2.75

☐ **LILA'S HAUNTED HOUSE PARTY # 23**   15919-4 $2.75

☐ **COUSIN KELLY'S FAMILY SECRET # 24**   15920-8 $2.75

☐ **LEFT-OUT ELIZABETH # 25**   15921-6 $2.99

☐ **JESSICA'S SNOBBY CLUB # 26**   15922-4 $2.99

☐ **THE SWEET VALLEY CLEANUP TEAM # 27**   15923-2 $2.99